D1326014

First published by Parragon in 2012
Parragon
Queen Street House
4 Queen Street
Bath BA1 1HE, UK
www.parragon.com

Copyright © 2012 Disney/Pixar
Porsche™; Mercury™; Model T™; FIAT™; ©Volkswagen AG; Chevrolet™; Mazda Miata™;
Jeep®; Sarge's rank insignia design used with the approval of the U.S. Army.
Slinky® Dog. © Poof-Slinky, Inc.; Mr. and Mrs. Potato Head® © Hasbro, Inc.

Edited by; Katrina Hanford
Designed by; Pete Hampshire
Production by; Emma Fulleylove

All rights reserved. No part of this publication may be reproduced, stored in a retrieval
system or transmitted, in any form or by any means, electronic, mechanical, photocopying,
recording or otherwise, without the prior permission of the copyright holder.

ISBN 978-1-4454-6500-5

Printed in China

Amazing
Adventure Stories

Parragon

Bath • New York • Singapore • Hong Kong • Cologne • Delhi
Melbourne • Amsterdam • Johannesburg • Auckland • Shenzhen

Contents

Disney·PIXAR
MONSTERS, INC.

A Place to Call Home

Lightning McQueen, a hotshot rookie race car, had just finished the most important race of his career. He hadn't come in first, but he had shown he was a car to watch.

Now, he was driving back to his new home in Radiator Springs with his friends. They had all gone to California to cheer him on.

Sheriff pulled up alongside Lightning as they drove. "We're mighty glad you've decided to stay in Radiator Springs," he said.

"Me, too," Lightning said. "I just don't want to spend any more time with Bessie," he joked. Bessie was a paving machine that Lightning had worked with to repave a portion of the local road he'd torn up.

Sheriff laughed. Then he said, "Bessie is an important member of town, too. Why, without her, our streets would still be dirt!"

Mater pulled up ahead of the other cars. "You can't turn as easy on dirt," he said as he drove in the shape of an eight. "And forget about driving backwards! I'm sure glad these roads are so smooth."

"Wow," Lightning said. "I didn't know Bessie had been here that long."

"Son, there's a lot you don't know about this town," Sheriff said. He began to tell Lightning about it.

A car named Stanley had been the first to cruise into the area. He decided to name the town Radiator Springs. When Lizzie rolled in years later, Stanley fell in love and asked her to stay and sell bumper stickers.

At first, Lizzie's shop was just a tent at the side of the road. As new cars began to settle in town, Lizzie and Stanley helped them open their own shops. Lizzie even moved into a building in the centre of town.

It seemed that just about every car that travelled that way stopped in Radiator Springs. The cars opened a tyre shop, a paint shop and a café, among many other shops. Anything a car wanted could be found in the friendly little town.

Then Sheriff explained how a wealthy and important car from Las Vegas had opened the Wheel Well Motel.

"That was some fancy motel," Sheriff said. "We even had the governor come spend the night. That's when we knew we were a proper town."

Lightning knew about the old motel. Sally had brought him up there to see the valley when he'd first come to Radiator Springs. He knew she'd loved the old building. As Sheriff continued to describe the town, Lightning wished he could have been there to see it then!

"Radiator Springs was the best stop on the mother road," Sheriff said.

"And you were here in town then?" Lightning asked.

"You bet!" Sheriff exclaimed. "With the town growing, I was hired to keep the riffraff under control."

"I hired Red, too," Sheriff continued. He glanced at the shy fire engine at the edge of the crowd of cars. "I knew we needed a firefighter and Red's about the most helpful truck I know."

The fire engine, who had been listening, blushed.

Sheriff chuckled. "Took some folks a while to realize that even though Red is so shy, he'll always be there when you need him."

"Mater rolled into town next," Sheriff continued.

"That's right!" the tow truck interrupted. "I was towing this car who'd blown a gasket and we heard there was a doctor here in town."

The cars turned to look at Doc Hudson. He sighed, then said, "After my racing days were over, I'd been looking for a town where I could slow down. Couldn't imagine a better place than here," he finished with a small smile.

Lightning listened eagerly as the other cars told their stories. He knew Sally, the shiny blue sports car, had been a lawyer in California. But he had never heard about Luigi's and Guido's boat ride all the way from Italy!

Flo had been a famous show car. She came to Radiator Springs while the Motorama Girls were travelling to their next show. She decided to stay in town after she met Ramone. They'd been cruising low and slow ever since.

17

"Wow," Lightning said once everyone had told their stories. The cars had made it back to town and were at Flo's V8 Café. After the long trip, they were ready for a sip of oil. "It's great that so many cars stopped here along the way and decided to stay."

The cars looked at one another. "See," Sally finally said, "Radiator Springs still is *the* stop on the mother road." She smiled. "The town just wouldn't be the same if we all hadn't ended up here."

Mater grinned. "I'm sure glad I stayed here. Where would I have opened Tow Mater's if I hadn't?"

Lizzie drove over to welcome everyone back home. "It was so quiet here without you. I started to think I'd have to find new cars to resettle in this town."

" 'Course not," Doc replied. "We took the long road home is all. But it's good to be back."

That night, the cars all gathered in town. They
thought about going to a drive-in movie or cruising the
streets to enjoy the neon lights. But instead, they parked
in front of Casa Della Tires and told more stories about
their lives before they rolled into town.

Lightning smiled as he listened to his friends tell their
tales. He was glad he'd found his way to Radiator Springs.
He couldn't think of a better place to call home.

Racing Days in Radiator Springs

One afternoon, the cars in Radiator Springs gathered eagerly at Flo's V8 Café. Lightning McQueen was meeting them there. He had some big news to share.

"Hey, guys," Lightning said when he rolled up, "thanks for meeting me. Doc and I wanted to tell you about our plans for the town. We want to open my racing headquarters here."

"That's right," Doc Hudson chimed in. He smiled. He was a racing legend and Lightning's new crew chief.

"There will be a real track and a large stadium to hold everyone who wants to come see a race," he explained.

Mater showed the cars a picture of what the stadium would look like.

"Hmm," said Sally, the shiny blue sports car. "This could be what puts Radiator Springs back on the map."

"That's the plan!" Lightning exclaimed.

It wasn't long before the track was ready. Lightning and Doc were excited. They decided to host a race to officially open the stadium.

They sent invitations to racers from around the world.
They wanted the opening race at Radiator Springs' stadium
to be a big event.

When the week of the race arrived, visitors flooded into town. The shop owners in Radiator Springs were very happy to have customers again. But they weren't prepared for so many!

A queue of cars waiting for new tyres stretched around the block at Casa Della Tires. Luigi and Guido had to work long after their normal closing time to help every car.

"Mamma mia!" Luigi said. "The cars, they just keep-a coming!"

The queue for Flo's V8 café stretched down the street. Her customers couldn't all fit into the car park, so she tried bringing cans of oil to them. But she couldn't get around the traffic and ended up spilling oil on her bonnet.

Meanwhile, Sheriff was having a hard time keeping the race cars in line.

Otto had come all the way from Germany. He was used to driving fast everywhere he went. But Sheriff wanted him to follow the speed limit.

When Sheriff gave Otto a speeding ticket, it didn't help. Otto just thought Sheriff wanted his autograph!

That night, Sally and Sarge had to set up tents for the visiting cars because her motel didn't have any more rooms.

By the time they were finished, Sally was exhausted.

"I'm glad we have visitors again, but I didn't think there would be this much work," she told Lightning.

The race car knew his friends were tired from a long day of taking care of so many customers. He suggested they take some time to have fun.

They decided to cruise through town. The neon lights were shining. Seeing the town lit up and full of visitors made everyone happy.

The next day, it was time for the Radiator Springs track's opening race.

Mater, Sarge, Sally, Lizzie and Flo gathered to watch from the box seats.

Down on the track, Lightning met his competition. He knew it would be a tough race. But he wanted to make his friends proud.

"And they're off!" Mater announced. The cars sped into their first turn.

"Lightning McQueen is in third place, but don't worry," the tow truck continued. "He'll win by the end. He's the best..."

"Mater," Sally interrupted, "you need to announce the positions of all the cars."

"But Lightning's my best friend," Mater said into the microphone. "And he's the best car in the race."

Down on the track, Lightning smiled. He revved his engine and soon he was level with Otto, who was in first place.

On the last turn, Lightning pulled ahead and Otto began to drop back!

Lightning stuck out his tongue as he crossed the finish line. He wanted to make sure he was the winner.

Mater cheered as he announced that his best friend had won.

"Thanks, everyone!" Lightning said to the crowd and the visiting race cars. "This was a great race, but it won't be the last here in Radiator Springs!"

The cars cheered. They couldn't wait until the next race!

Guido's
Big Surprise

Luigi was bursting with excitement. He was planning a racing-themed surprise party for his assistant and best friend, Guido. They were both big racing fans.

Guido rolled to a stop beside his friend outside Casa Della Tires.

"Today is-a going to be a good-a day, eh, Guido?" Luigi said.

The little forklift sighed. Then he turned and went into the shop, ready to get to work.

Luigi chuckled. "He has-a no idea! My friend is-a in for a big-a surprise."

Just then, Ramone pulled up. "Hey, man, I'm here for my new tyres," he said.

"Perfecto!" Luigi exclaimed. "Come on-a inside."

"Has Guido figured out the surprise?" Ramone whispered before they went in.

"No, it's-a still a secret," Luigi replied.

Luigi and Ramone went inside. "Guido," Luigi said, "Signore Ramone is here for his-a new tyres."

Guido went into the back room to get them.

"How is your-a lovely lady, Flo?" Luigi asked Ramone.

"She's doing fine," Ramone said as Guido reappeared. "She just got a new shipment of fuel that is mighty smooth. You should stop in for a sip."

"Yes, maybe we'll-a come over later." Luigi winked at Ramone. He knew that the surprise party would take place at Flo's V8 Café. Then he noticed the tyres Guido had found. Two were flat and the other two were covered with mud.

"Guido," Luigi said slowly, "I put those-a tyres in the junk pile this-a morning."

The little forklift looked at the tyres he was holding and his eyes widened. He hurried back to the storeroom.

"He looks blue, man," Ramone said.

Luigi frowned. "Of course he looks-a blue. He is *always* the colour blue."

Ramone laughed. "No, I meant that Guido looks sad."

When Guido returned with the correct tyres, Luigi watched him. Guido did look sad. Luigi hoped the party would cheer him up.

"What's-a bugging you, Guido?" Luigi asked later.

But the only response was a loud, "Ka-chow!" as Lightning McQueen rolled into the shop, followed by Mater.

"Hey, guys," said Lightning, "I'm here to practise for my next big race. You'll be my pit crew again. Right, Guido?"

The forklift nodded.

"Here's the plan," Lightning said. "Picture me speeding down the track. You be ready for the pit stop, okay?"

"He's-a ready," Luigi answered.

Guido got into his pit stop position.

Vroom. "I'm heading for the pit stop," Lightning pretended, "and you're ready to change my tyres in 2.5 seconds flat. And... go!"

Guido set to work. Luigi and Mater counted. But Guido was working very slowly.

"Two and a half-a," Luigi said, drawing out the numbers. "Three-a...."

"Three, four, five," Mater counted.

It took Guido five seconds – double his usual time!

"Mamma mia!" Luigi exclaimed. "Uh... Guido didn't sleep-a so good last night. Tomorrow, he will be back to his-a speedy self."

Lightning nodded, but he looked worried. He turned and followed Mater out of the shop.

"Hey, buddy, what would our country be called if every car was painted pink?" the tow truck said. He barely paused before shouting, "'A pink carnation!' Get it, 'car' and 'nation'?"

Luigi turned to his friend. "What's-a wrong, Guido?" he asked. "You cannot go on being down in the dumpster."

"Hello, boys," Sally said as she rolled in. "There's a customer at my motel who needs her tyres checked. Do you have some time?"

Guido perked up a little. He went to grab his toolbox.

"Guido will take-a good care of her," Luigi said.

Sally smiled. "I knew I could count on you guys. Come on, Guido. I'll take you over to meet her." Then she turned back to Luigi and said, "I'm heading over to Flo's afterwards if you need me."

"Grazie, Sally," Luigi replied.

Luigi's

CASA DELLA TIRES

After Guido left, Luigi circled the shop, cleaning things up. He saw a wrench lying on the floor and went to put it with the rest of Guido's tools. When Luigi opened the chest, he saw a postcard from Italy. It was from Guido's cousin, Guidoni.

Luigi gasped. "Guido is-a homesick! That's-a why he's so sad."

Luigi put the wrench and the card in the chest. Then he raced over to Flo's. They had to change their racing-themed surprise party to a grand Italian celebration.

Flo was serving drinks to Lightning, Sally, Mater and Ramone at her café when Luigi appeared.

"He's-a sick!" Luigi exclaimed.

The other cars gathered around him. "Who's sick?" Sally asked.

"Guido!" Luigi cried. "He's-a homesick for his family in Italy. I thought he was-a missing the excitement of a race. But now I'm sure he's been sad because he misses his-a home."

"Well," said Sally, "Guido has a home right here in Radiator Springs – and we're going to cheer him up."

"That's right," said Flo. "We'll just change our racing party to an Italian party! I'll see if Fillmore has an olive oil flavoured brew. That would be perfecto."

Lightning smiled. "You can count on me to bring Italian racing flags for decorations."

"And Flo's got some old Italian classics on the car-aoke machine," Ramone chimed in. "'Lugnut Prima' is one of our favourites."

Luigi smiled as his friends piped up with more ideas for the party. "Grazie," Luigi said. "This will mean-a so much to Guido."

Luigi left Flo, Sally and Ramone at the café to keep planning, while he went with Lightning and Mater to find Red the fire engine. They had a great idea for a big finale.

Luckily, Red agreed. He couldn't wait to be part of the surprise.

That night, Luigi could barely contain his excitement. "It's-a been a long day, eh, Guido," he said. "What do you say we go over to Flo's for a sip of oil?"

Guido gave a little nod, then followed Luigi out the door.

When they arrived at Flo's, all of the inside lights were off. It looked like the café was closed.

"I wonder what's-a going on?" Luigi said, trying to hide a smile. "Let's go in and see."

As soon as they rolled into the café, the lights came on. "Viva Italiano, Guido!" Flo said. The other cars all cheered.

Guido looked around in awe. There were Italian flags hanging on the walls, and lots of red, white and green balloons filled the café.

There were posters of famous Italian landmarks. Mater stopped beside the one of the Leaning Tower of Tyres. "Hey, this here picture looks a lot like the tower outside Luigi's shop," he said.

Mater rolled up to the front of the café. "Can I have everyone's attention, please?"

Ramone dimmed the lights until a single spotlight shone on the tow truck.

"Now for a real surprise," he said. "Red will perform an Italian opera selection."

Red shyly moved into the spotlight. Flo started up the car-aoke machine. Beautiful music filled the air and Red began to sing.

"Mamma mia!" Luigi said. "It's bellissimo."

Guido closed his eyes as he listened. He felt like he was back home in Italy listening to opera with his family.

When Red finished, all the cars were speechless. The fire engine quickly moved out of the spotlight.

"Red, that was just beautiful," Sally said.

"You made this-a night so very special," Luigi said.

Red smiled shyly.

Flo set to work making sure everyone had enough oil. Mater told Red and Lightning some more jokes.

Luigi pulled his friend aside. "You are-a happy again now?" he asked Guido.

The little forklift beamed and waved an Italian flag. There was no need to be homesick when he was already right at home in Radiator Springs.

Rumble at the Rust Bucket

It was opening day at Rust Bucket Stadium. Cars of all makes, shapes and sizes were driving into the stands.

Mater drove into the stadium with his best friend, Lightning McQueen. "Welcome to my new stadium," said the tow truck. "Now you're not the only one with a fancy new place to play. We can do all kinds of stuff here."

"Wow, this is amazing," said Lightning as he rolled to a stop. He looked around. "I've never been in a stadium like this before!"

"That's because this is the very first stadium that I ever owned and designed," Mater replied.

The crowd began to cheer as Mater swung his tow hook in the air like a lasso.

"Welcome, cars, trucks and vans to Rust Bucket Stadium," he hollered. "Where a truck can be a truck. Now it's time for some tyre-snagging!"

Mater grabbed the first tyre with his hook.

Suddenly, an engine roared. VROOM! It grew louder and louder!

"That sounds like Bubba," Mater said.

Bubba was a big orange tow truck who made a racket wherever he went. He liked to bully smaller trucks into doing anything he wanted. He smiled as he pulled into the stadium with his friends Tater and Tater Junior.

"Last time I saw him, he tried to take my bonnet," Mater whispered to Lightning. "But I outsmarted that big truck!"

"Mater!" exclaimed Bubba. "I think it's time for us to find out who is the best tow truck around. I challenge you to a truck derby. The winner gets to keep the Rust Bucket!"

"You're on!" Mater cried. "No tow truck is greater than Mater."

"All right, Bubba," Lightning said, "if you beat Mater, you win the Rust Bucket. But if Mater wins, you can't come back to the stadium, or to Radiator Springs. Deal?"

"Deal," said Bubba. "If I lose, I'll never set one tyre in Carburetor County ever again."

"Uhh... Lightning," Mater said, "if I lose, can I stay in Radiator Springs? This is my home and . . ."

"Mater," Lightning said with a smile, "of course you can stay in town. But try to beat Bubba so he leaves!"

Mater and Bubba agreed to compete in three events: tyre-snagging, cone-dodging and a one-lap race around a dirt track. Whoever won

RUST BUCKET
CHAMPION

the most events would be the Rust Bucket champion!

Lightning gave his friend some last-minute encouragement. "Remember, Mater, you're quicker than quick. And you're the world's best backwards driver! Go and show Bubba what you're made of!"

"All right, buddy," Mater said.

The two tow trucks faced each other, bonnet-to-bonnet.

"We're going to need judges for this competition," said Bubba. "And my pals Tater and Tater Junior will be perfect."

"We get to be judges?" said Tater Junior. "That's terrific!"

"I can't wait to tell all my friends at the garage!" Tater said.

Lightning was worried about letting Bubba's friends be the judges. But Mater was sure he could win, no matter what.

"All right, boys, you've got the job," said Mater. "Go on up to the judges' stand so we can get this thing started."

Tyre-snagging was the first event. Guido balanced a huge stack of tyres on his lift and waited for the signal.

"Let the tyre-snagging begin!" shouted Tater Junior.

Guido threw the tyres into the air. Both tow trucks used their cables and hooks to snag as many tyres as they could.

Mater quickly snagged four tyres. But Bubba was fast, too. He hooked four as well.

Bubba didn't want Mater to win. When he saw that they were tied, he used his hook to knock a tyre away from Mater.

The rest of the tyres hit the ground and the event was over. The judges took a quick count.

"Mater has three tyres," said Tater Junior. "But Bubba has four. Bubba wins!"

"But he cheated!" Lightning yelled. He turned to the judges. "Didn't you see that?"

Tater shook his head. "Sorry, we must have missed it," he said.

Next up was cone-dodging. Mater and Bubba slowly pulled up to the starting line.

"You're going down," growled Bubba.

"Doubt it!" replied Mater. He looked out over the track where cones were set up for the trucks to drive around. Mater had raced around this track plenty of times.

At the signal, Mater and Bubba took off.

"*Yee-haw!*" yelled Mater as he edged ahead of Bubba. He weaved around the cones with ease.

The big truck couldn't stay on the track. Bubba kept sliding when he tried to turn in the dust.

The dust didn't bother Mater, though. When he slid, he just turned around and drove backwards. He moved between the cones and didn't hit a single one!

The crowd went wild when Mater crossed the finish line first. Bubba was still on the track, coughing up dust and surrounded by cones.

"Mater wins!" said Tater Junior.

Mater and Bubba rolled up to the starting line for the last race. Bubba wasn't happy. He didn't like to lose.

"You won that one, but you'll never beat me in an all-out race!" said Bubba as he revved his engine.

"May the best truck win," said Mater.

"I will!" Bubba yelled.

The race started and the trucks sped off. Bubba used his powerful engine to pull ahead of Mater. Then he dropped his hook and cable to the ground and let it drag behind him. He really wanted to win this event.

"Watch out, Mater!" yelled Lightning.

Mater dodged the sharp hook swinging across the road in front of him.

Suddenly, Bubba's hook got caught on a rock! Bubba was jerked back into the air, where he flipped and landed on his side.

"Oww! Help me!" he cried.

Mater slammed on his brakes.

"Hold on, Bubba! I'll get you back on your tyres in a jiffy," he said.

Mater swung his tow cable towards Bubba and latched it onto his roof. He pulled and pulled with all his might. But the big truck was too heavy for him to flip over. Then Mater had an idea.

"Tater! Tater Junior! Get over here!" yelled Mater. "I need your help lifting Bubba!"

The three tow trucks used their hooks to pull Bubba off his side and set him back on all four tyres.

"Nice teamwork!" said Lightning as the crowd cheered. Tater and Tater Junior smiled.

"Thanks," muttered Bubba. Then he drove out of the stadium, embarrassed.

"Well, I guess that makes you the winner," said Tater Junior.

The crowd cheered for Mater – the Rust Bucket champion!

"Uh, Mr Tow Mater," said Tater, "can you teach us a few of your tricks?"

"Sure!" replied Mater.

Guido tossed some tyres into the air. Mater coached the tow trucks until they got it. They soon found out it was harder than it looked!

All's Well at the
Wheel Well

Radiator Springs was bustling with activity. The grand reopening of the Wheel Well Motel was in less than a week.

Sally the shiny blue sports car was very excited. Ever since the famous race car, Lightning McQueen, had moved his racing headquarters to Radiator Springs, the town had been filled with visitors. When all the rooms at the Cozy Cone Motel had been booked for weeks and weeks, Sally decided it was time to reopen the Wheel Well.

"Radiator Springs is back on the map," she had told her friends. "Now, we need another motel for all the cars that visit."

The townsfolk had agreed with Sally. They were happy to see visitors return to the town. And they were eager to help Sally fix up the old motel.

"We'll be the most popular place in Carburetor County!" Sally cheered.

Ramone helped Sally decorate the rooms inside the motel. He gave each one its own style. "Then cars will want to return to check out the different looks," the hot rod explained.

Sally's favourite was a room overlooking the valley. Ramone had painted a mural of Radiator Springs at night, showing the shops with their neon lights.

"This is great, Ramone!" Sally exclaimed. "My two favourite views are in one room."

While Ramone fixed up the inside of the motel, Red helped Sally spruce up the outside.

The fire engine had created new flower displays for the motel. He watered each patch once a day and drove out to the motel at least twice more to make sure everything looked perfect for the grand reopening.

When Lightning McQueen rolled back into town, he found Mater, Flo and Sheriff at Flo's V8 Café.

"Welcome back, buddy," the tow truck said with a wide smile. "We sure missed you around here."

"Thanks, Mater. I'm glad to be home," Lightning said. He had been travelling to different events in the past few weeks. But no matter how many trophies he won, he was always eager to get back to Radiator Springs. "I love racing, but it's nice to slow down every now and then."

"Well, you don't have much time before things speed up here," Flo told him. "Sally's opening the new Wheel Well in just three days."

"Really? Is she ready? Maybe I should go out there and see if she needs any help," Lightning said.

"I'll race you!" Mater exclaimed. "Last one there has to clean my wheel wells!"

A few minutes later, Lightning skidded to a stop in front of the Wheel Well. He was just ahead of Mater.

"Aw, shucks," Mater said. "I almost had you."

"Next time I'll race you driving backwards. You'll win for sure," Lightning replied. He looked up at the motel. "Wow, Sally really has fixed this place up."

"Everybody helped," Mater said. "I got to tow old shrubs out of the way so Red could plant the new flowers. And I promised Miss Sally I would give all her customers free backwards driving lessons!"

The two cars rolled over to Guido and Luigi. They'd brought some tyres out from Luigi's shop, Casa Della Tires. Guido was creating a new tyre display for the reopening.

"You are just in-a time," Luigi said, when he saw the race car and tow truck. "Guido is almost-a finished."

Guido put the last tyre into place. Then he rolled back to admire his work.

"It's a wheel... made of wheels," Lightning said slowly.

"That's-a right!" Luigi said proudly.

"Hey, Stickers," Sally said as she drove over. "When did you get back to town?"

"Just a little while ago," Lightning replied. "This place looks great, Sally. Is there anything I can do to help you get ready?"

"You've already done more than enough," Sally said. "You brought customers back to our town by setting up your racing headquarters here." She smiled and went to check on one of the rooms.

"Miss Sally sure does like you," Mater said to his friend. "Whoo-eee!"

"Oh, come on, Mater. Sally's just excited about reopening the motel. I wish I could think of something to do to make the day even more special for her," Lightning said. "I'm gonna go for a drive. Maybe that will help me think."

"Okay, buddy," Mater said. "Just remember to keep your wheels on the road!"

Lightning drove down the mountain and through the valley. He passed the old dirt track he used to practise on. He slowed down as he rolled into the centre of town.

The cars that weren't helping out at the Wheel Well were getting their shops ready for the extra customers who would come for the reopening. Lightning saw Lizzie out in front of her shop, Radiator Springs Curios. He rolled over to say hello.

"Stanley would have gotten all steamed up if he could see the town today," Lizzie said. "Why, the Wheel Well was one of his favourite spots!"

Lizzie slapped a sticker on Lightning's front bumper and went back to tidying up her shop.

Lightning looked at the bumper sticker in a reflection on an old hubcap. It read: ALL'S WELL AT THE WHEEL WELL. He smiled. Lizzie always had the perfect sticker.

Lightning left Lizzie, but he couldn't stop thinking of what she'd said about Stanley, who had founded the town. If only he could see Radiator Springs today!

Then he thought about what Sally had said – that he'd been the one to bring visitors back to town.

"All because of a little racing," he murmured. Suddenly, he had an idea!

A race car couldn't paint rooms at the motel or sell stickers. But he could help Sally make headlines at the opening with a trick or two. He zoomed off to tell Sally his idea – and to start practising.

For the next two days, Lightning worked on his trick.

Mater drove out to the old track and watched him take turn after turn. "You're up to something!" he called out to his friend.

Lightning only smiled and kept practising.

The morning of the grand reopening, the cars from Radiator Springs were gathered in front of the Wheel Well with press cars and visitors. Everyone was excited. The cars oohed and aahed over the motel.

"Ladies and gentlecars," Sally greeted everyone. "It is my pleasure to welcome you to the historic Wheel Well Motel, once again open to all the travellers who come to Radiator Springs. And now, to kick off the festivities, Lightning McQueen would like to give you an official Wheel Well welcome!"

There was a loud vroom. Lightning zipped around the press cars. When he was right in front of Sally, he turned and lifted his two left wheels at the same time to wave to the crowd.

The press cars snapped photos and the crowd cheered loudly.

Then Lightning looped around Sally and waved with his two right wheels.

The crowd went wild.

A few minutes later, Sally invited everyone inside for a tour. She stood by the door and welcomed each car.

When Lightning pulled up beside her, she smiled. "You really got the crowd excited about the motel. You care about this town a lot."

Lightning beamed. "Getting lost here was the best thing that ever happened to me," he said. "It's my home."

Sally looked at the bumper sticker on Lightning's front fender. "Nice sticker," she said as she rolled inside.

Lightning laughed as he followed her. All was well at the Wheel Well... and in Radiator Springs.

Deputy Mater

Early one morning, Sally the shiny blue sports car was busy working at the Cozy Cone Motel. She'd had a lot of customers lately. Radiator Springs was full of visiting cars hoping to catch a glimpse of Lightning McQueen!

Sally heard a loud vroom outside. "Lightning must be back from his latest race," she said to herself. She rolled outside to welcome him home.

But Lightning wasn't the one revving his engine. Three tricked-out cars with loud engines – and even louder radios – zoomed through town.

Sally didn't like to see other cars ruining the peace and quiet. She drove over to Flo's V8 Café to see if anyone else had seen – or heard – the fancy cars zipping through town.

She found Sheriff and Fillmore at the café. Sheriff was trying to explain why the traffic light only flashed yellow.

"That tells cars to drive carefully," Sheriff said. "They should slow down, but they don't have to stop if there's no other traffic."

"Good morning," Sally said. "Did you see those cars that just raced through town? They could use a lesson in traffic laws!"

"I've seen those cars around before," Sheriff said. "I haven't been able to catch them yet. They don't follow the speed limit and I bet they don't even know we have a traffic light in town."

Sally and Sheriff drove down Main Street. They wanted to see if any other cars had seen the speeders.

"Oh, no!" Sally said when they saw Red, the shy fire engine. He was looking at his garden. The speeding cars had run over the flowers! "Those cars have ruined Red's garden!"

"I know, Sally," Sheriff said with a sigh. "But I can't be everywhere in town at one time."

Sally agreed. Tracking down cars who wouldn't follow the town's driving rules was a big job. With all the tourists coming through, Sheriff had been busier than ever!

"What if we helped?" Sally said. "You could name some cars as deputies. They could watch over certain places in town when you can't be there."

"That's a great idea!" Fillmore said. "I bet lots of cars would be willing to help."

"Howdy, folks," Mater called out as he drove towards them. "What's rolling down Main Street? Besides me!"

The tow truck laughed loudly.

"Mater, why are your sides white?" Sally asked.

"Oh, shoot," Mater said. "I asked Ramone if he could patch up my rusty spots and he had the wrong paint in the sprayer."

"Looks like the perfect spot for a sticker," Fillmore said.

"Or... a deputy badge!" Sally said. "Mater, would you want to help Sheriff catch any rule-breakers who come through town?"

"Me?" Mater asked. "Why sure, Miss Sally. I've always wanted to stop ruler-breaking. I...."

"No, Mater," Sheriff interrupted. "As a deputy, you'll be on the lookout for rule-breaker cars who can't follow the speed limit or obey the laws of our town."

Mater was eager to start helping Sheriff!

Sally rounded up all the cars in town. They gathered at the courthouse, where Sheriff made Mater an honorary deputy.

Then, Mater was allowed to choose some other cars to help him. He picked Sally, Sarge and Lightning McQueen. They were made honorary deputies, too.

After all of Mater's deputies were sworn in, Ramone painted a Radiator Springs badge on their doors. Then the cars set to work.

Mater assigned each deputy an area to watch over. Lightning kept an eye on the intersection with the blinking yellow light. He was right across the street from Flo's. She had extra cans of oil at the ready for all the new deputies.

Sarge took up a position near Lightning. He used his long-range binoculars to look for cars approaching the town.

Sally drove around to all the shops. She chatted with the owners to make sure they were happy with their customers.

The town was quiet and peaceful – just the way the cars wanted it!

Mater drove through town, keeping an eye out for rule-breaking cars. He also checked in with each of his deputies.

"This is a tough job," he told Lightning. "But I'm just the tow truck to do it!"

Lightning smiled. His friend was doing a great job. There hadn't been any sign of trouble in town for the whole day!

Suddenly, they heard Sarge call out, "Incoming! Speeding cars approaching town!"

All the deputies gathered on Main Street. Mater rolled to the front of the crowd.

The cars could feel the thump of loud music through their tyres. They waited for the visitors to come into view.

"They're the same cars that sped through here the other day," Sally whispered to Lightning.

"We'll stop them this time, Sally," Lightning assured her. "Deputy Mater's ready to tell those cars who's in charge."

The tricked-out cars rolled to a stop in front of Mater.

"Howdy, out-of-towners," Mater greeted them. "We're glad to have you visit. But we've had some complaints that you aren't following our rules."

The car with the radio turned down his music. "What rules?" he asked.

"Well, see, we have a speed limit here," Mater said. "And your radio is so loud, I can't hear my own engine clunking."

"Isn't that the speed limit?" one of the cars asked. He pointed towards the '66' posted at the side of the road.

Mater looked at the sign. He chuckled. Then he burst out laughing. "That does look like a speed limit sign," he said. "But it's really the route number of the road you're driving on. And this little town is the nicest stop you'll find in all of Carburetor County."

"Anyhow," Mater continued, "this little light is more

important than the speed limit."

Mater swung his tow hook up to the blinking yellow traffic light.

"Sheriff told me that this means slow down," Mater said. "So whenever you see a yellow light, hit the brakes before you break the rules."

"That sounds easy enough," one of the cars said. The others agreed.

Mater invited the out-of-towners to stay for a can of oil at Flo's. The cars followed Mater slowly down the street to the café.

All the deputies joined them. They'd had fun helping Sheriff keep order in town. And now they were ready to celebrate a job well done!

REMATCH!

Lightning McQueen and Francesco Bernoulli had challenged each other to a race in Monza, Italy – Francesco's hometown.

"Benvenuto!" said Francesco. "Your plane was late, but this is no surprise. You will be late crossing the finish line, too."

Lightning smiled. Then he whispered to Mater, "I am so beating him – right here on his own turf!"

As they left the airport, the cars were surrounded by photographers.

"Everyone loves Francesco. He has too many fans," said Francesco.

"Nobody has more fans than
Lightning!" Mater piped up.
Francesco rolled his eyes.
"We will prove it!" said Luigi.
"Lightning gets hundreds of fan letters each day.
Guido, bring the postbags!"
Guido zoomed off!

109

Guido returned with postbags overflowing with fan letters.
Lightning was a little embarrassed. "Oh, it's really not
that big of a deal," he said.

"You are right, Lightning," said Francesco. "It is no big deal because Francesco has much, much more fan mail!"

"Letters are great," said Lightning. "But we like to get
some bumper-to-bumper time with our fans whenever we can."

Lightning and his friends greeted all the cars who were
queued up to see them.

Mater really got the fans going. They began chanting.

"Light-NING! Light-NING!"

"Questo e' ridicolo!" mumbled Francesco. "And what about autographs?" he asked. "Watch – and be amazed."

Francesco started spinning his wheels and spewing out

hundreds of autographed photos of himself to his fans.
"See? Francesco always gets things done at three hundred
kilometres an hour."

After the two racers finished greeting their fans, they drove to a café.

"Hey, Mr Francesco, nobody drinks oil faster than Lightning," said Mater.

"What?" said Lightning. "Mater, I can't drink...."

"C'mon buddy, show 'em what I done taught you!" said Mater.

Lightning sighed and managed to finish a can of oil in a few gulps.

Francesco was not impressed. "Francesco never guzzles," he said. "Oil should be savoured."

Lightning cruised over to Francesco. "How about a warm-up before the big race – just you and me?" he asked.

Francesco nodded. "Ah, good idea, Lightning! Try to keep up, if you...."

Before Francesco could finish, Lightning was a red
streak down the road!

"Ka-ciao, Francesco!" called Lightning.

Francesco was just about to catch up with Lightning when he nearly spun out on a left turn.

"How do you make those left turns so well?"
Francesco asked Lightning.

"Get equipped with some treaded tyres," said Lightning. "Then turn right to go left. A very good friend taught me that once."

They finally stopped to rest.

Francesco sighed. "Ahh, Italia is beautiful, no? Just like
Francesco!"

Lightning chuckled. "Do you always think about
yourself?" he asked.

"Of course," said Francesco. "On the racetrack, Francesco
only thinks about himself and doing his best. This is why he
always wins!"

The next day was the big race. Finally, the world would find out who was the fastest race car! When the flag dropped, the fans went wild!

Francesco came out of the first left turn ahead of Lightning. He showed off his new treaded tyres. "Perhaps Lightning has taught Francesco too well!"

Lightning couldn't help but smile.

The racers entered the Monza arena and made a pit stop. As Lightning zoomed out of the pits, he got distracted by the camera flashes and the screaming fans. Suddenly Lightning remembered what Francesco had said about focusing on himself and doing his best. Lightning looked straight ahead and took the lead!

As the two cars crossed the finish line, the crowd gasped.

"Ka-chow!" yelled Lightning. "I won!"

"You mean ciao bella," said Francesco. "Francesco won!"

The truth stunned everyone. According to the judges, the race was a... TIE!!!

The cars tried to figure out what to do.

Then Francesco shouted, "No more talk! Talk is slow.

What do we do? We race!"

"That's a great idea!" said Lightning. "We'll race in Radiator Springs!"

Then the two fastest cars in the world zoomed away together... to race again another day.

Disney·PIXAR
MONSTERS, INC.

Late at night, a little boy awoke to see... a monster! He screamed! Then, the monster screamed, too!

With a sigh, the teacher turned off the mechanical boy. Then she repeated the rules: Never scream. And NEVER leave a child's cupboard door open. Why?

"It could let in a child!" bellowed Mr Waternoose, the CEO of Monsters, Incorporated.

The Scarers-in-Training gasped. They knew that children's screams powered Monstropolis. But letting a child into the world of monsters would be deadly to everyone!

Meanwhile, across town, James P. Sullivan was exercising.
His assistant (and best friend), Mike Wazowski, was
coaching him.

Sulley was a professional Scarer
and he needed to keep in top shape.

"Feel the burn," Mike urged. "You
call yourself a monster?!"

At Monsters, Inc., Sulley was famous for collecting more screams than anyone else.

That was important because the city was having an energy shortage. Human kids were getting harder to scare and Monstropolis needed all the screams it could get.

In the locker room, a monster named Randall popped
out at Mike.

"AHHH!" Mike shrieked.

Randall was creepy and mean... and very jealous of
Sulley. Randall would do anything to be the top Scarer.

It was time for the workday to begin. As other workers watched in awe, Sulley led all the Scarers of Monsters, Inc. onto the Scare Floor. Together, these were the best scream collectors in the business. As the Scarers prepared for work, a conveyor belt dropped a door at each station. When the red signal flashed, each Scarer would walk through his door – and into the room of a sleeping child.

Hopefully, the child would let out a good scream!

When work was finished, Mike rushed to meet his girlfriend, Celia. They had planned a special date.

But the company's cranky file clerk blocked Mike's way. "I'm sure you filed your paperwork," Roz rasped.

Mike had forgotten! Luckily, Sulley offered to help.

Back at the Scare Floor, Sulley noticed that someone had left a door behind, its red light still on. Puzzled, Sulley peeked through the door, but saw no one.

So he closed the door. Then he saw...
A CHILD!

"AAAAH!" he screamed.

At a restaurant, Mike and Celia were enjoying a romantic dinner. Mike was just telling Celia what a beautiful monster she was...when suddenly, he spotted Sulley waving frantically outside the restaurant window.

Sulley looked terrified.

Quickly, Sulley explained about the child. Mike was horrified... especially when Sulley showed him the girl! Then it began running around the restaurant! When the CDA arrived, Mike and Sulley hid the kid in a takeaway box and ran. They were in big trouble!

Back in their home, Sulley and Mike tried not to touch the child.

Then Mike accidentally fell and the little girl started to giggle. Strangely, her laughter made the lights burn brighter and brighter – until they burned out with a POP!

Finally, Sulley put the child to bed. But she was afraid. Sulley realized she was terrified that Randall was in the cupboard. So Sulley stayed with her until she fell asleep.

"This might sound crazy," Sulley told Mike, "but I don't think that kid is dangerous."

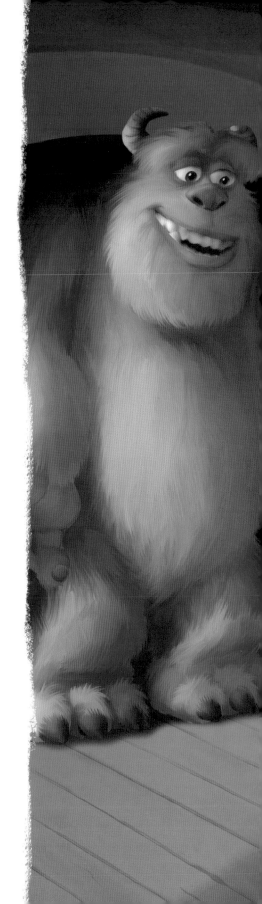

"What if we just put her back in her door?" Sulley wondered. Mike didn't like the idea, but what else could they do? The next morning, they disguised her and took her to work. The disguise fooled everyone!

In the locker room, Sulley and the child played hide-and-seek. "Boo!" she said playfully. Sulley was starting to really like her. But then they overheard Randall tell his assistant that he planned to 'take care of the kid'. Sulley needed to get the child home quickly!

But Mike made a mistake. "This isn't Boo's door," Sulley exclaimed.

"Boo?!?" Mike couldn't believe Sulley had named the kid.

Boo had a nickname for Sulley, too: 'Kitty'.

Oops, everyone could hear! So they began singing, instead. Meanwhile, where was Boo? She had slipped away! Mike and Sulley split up to find her, but Randall cornered Mike. The nasty monster knew all about Boo. He ordered Mike to bring her to the Scare Floor. He said he'd have her door ready.

After Sulley found Boo, Mike told him about Randall's plan. Together, they went to the Scare Floor, but Sulley was still worried. "We can't trust Randall!"

Mike disagreed. To prove the open door was safe, he went right through – and was captured by Randall!

Sulley and Boo followed Randall. They learned that he had invented a cruel new way to capture screams from kids. And he was about to try it out on Mike!

Sulley rescued Mike and then raced towards the training room. He needed to warn Mr Waternoose about Randall.

But in the training room, Boo accidentally saw Sulley looking ferocious. She was terrified!

Sulley felt awful. For the first time, he realized how mean it was to scare a child.

Mr Waternoose promised to fix everything, but he was really working with Randall!

Then Mr Waternoose shoved Sulley and Mike through a door into the human world. They were banished to the Himalayan mountains!

Sulley knew Boo was in trouble. He had to get back! Racing to the local village, he found a cupboard that could lead him home.

Then he rushed to Randall's secret lab. Sulley tore the machine apart.

As Sulley raced away with Boo, Mike arrived to help. But Celia couldn't understand what was going on. Quickly, Mike explained about Boo and about Randall's dastardly plan. When Celia saw Randall chasing Boo, she knew Mike was telling the truth.

Mike and Sulley climbed onto the machine that carried doors to the Scare Floor.

The power wasn't on, so Mike made a funny face. When Boo laughed, the power surged! The doors began to move!

But to send Boo home, they still needed to find her door.

The trio jumped in and out of cupboards, until at last, Randall grabbed Boo. Suddenly, Boo fought back! "She's not scared of you anymore," Sulley told Randall. Working together, they beat Randall once and for all.

Sulley, Mike and Boo weren't safe yet. Now Waternoose and the CDA were controlling the doors. While Mike distracted the CDA, Sulley escaped with Boo. Unfortunately, Waternoose saw everything. "Give me the child!" he yelled, running after Sulley.

But luckily, Mike recorded Waternoose yelling, "I'll kidnap a thousand children before I let this company die!"

Now all of Monstropolis knew that Waternoose planned to steal children. He was arrested by the head of the CDA – who turned out to be Roz!

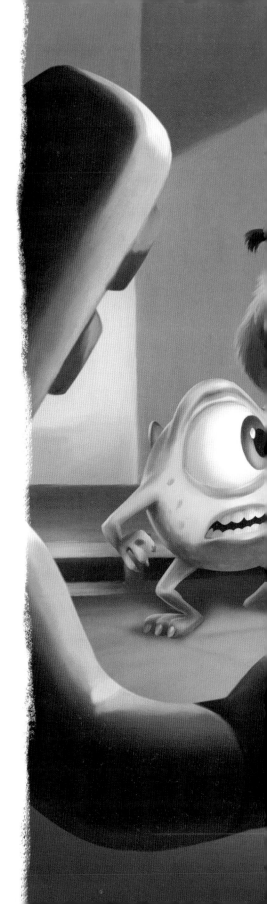

It was time for Boo to go home. Sulley followed her into her room. Gently, he tucked her into bed.

Sadly, Sulley returned to Monstropolis. Roz ordered the CDA to shred Boo's door. It couldn't be used for scaring anymore.

After that, Sulley became president of Monsters, Inc. And the Scare Floor became a Laugh Floor! It was all because Sulley had discovered that laughter produced more power than screams.

Monsters, Inc. and Monstropolis were saved.

Sulley still missed Boo, though. He had one tiny sliver of her door, but the rest had been destroyed by the CDA.

Before long, however, Mike surprised his pal. He'd put the door back together! It was missing just one little piece.

Sulley inserted the piece, opened the door and saw...

"Boo?" Sulley whispered.

"Kitty!" an excited voice replied.

The two friends were reunited at last.

BUZZ OFF

The toys were buzzing with excitement. Bonnie was going to the park with Woody, Jessie and Dolly. The others were looking forward to a day of fun in Bonnie's room.

Only Jessie was worried. "Keep an eye on Buzz," she whispered to her friends. "He's been acting funny. I think he may have a loose wire."

"No problem-o, Jessie," Hamm said.

Just then, Bonnie rushed into her room. "This is going to be so much fun!" she said, grabbing her backpack.

"Time to go, Bonnie!" her mother called from the car.

"Buzz, you're in charge now," Bonnie said as she left. "Keep things under control, okay?"

As soon as the coast was clear, the Peas began bouncing on their shelf. "Let's play!" they shouted.

"Oooo!" said an Alien.

Buzz stood up. "Wait!" he said. "This looks dangerous."

"What did you say, Buzz?" Slinky asked. Looking down at Buzz, he slipped and plunged halfway over the edge, causing an avalanche of Aliens and Peas. *Squeak, squeak, plunk, plunk, plunk!* They tumbled on top of Buzz!

Buzz stood up. He looked around. "Donde esta mi nave?" he asked.

"Great," Mr Potato Head observed. "The return of Señor Space Nut."

"Yup," Hamm agreed. "He's definitely switched into Spanish mode."

"What do we do?" Trixie asked. "Can we fix him?"

"Sure, we can... maybe," Hamm added. "Rex, see if you can put those tiny fingers to use and jiggle any loose wires you see."

But as Rex reached for Buzz, the space ranger dodged him. He didn't want anyone fiddling with his back panel!

"Catch him!" shouted Hamm, leading the other toys.

Buzz grabbed a curtain from the dollhouse and held it up like a bullfighter's cape. As the others slowly tried to surround him, Buzz stepped deftly from side to side, wildly flapping the curtain.

"Buzz, hold on," Slinky said calmly. "You're not yourself."

"Someone's going to get hurt!" cried Rex.

"I'll grab that curtain before he hits someone in the noggin!"
Hamm said as he ran to tackle his friend. But Buzz stepped aside,
snapping his red cape! Hamm skidded and kept sliding....

"Olé!" Trixie said, clapping with excitement.

171

CRASH! Hamm slid right into the bookshelf and flipped into the air. As the toys looked on in horror, a single book fell on its side and teetered precariously over Buzz's head.

"Buzz, look out!" Rex screamed. It was too late. The book fell right onto Buzz!

Silence fell over the room as the toys gathered around Buzz. Was he... broken? For a moment, nothing moved. Suddenly, a hand reached around the cover and Buzz pushed the book away.

"Buzz, are you okay?" Rex cried.

"Buzz, are you okay?" Buzz cried.

"Hey!" Rex turned to Hamm. "That's what I just said!"

Buzz blinked at Rex. "Hey! That's what I just said."

"No, that's what I said," Rex explained.

Hamm whispered to Buttercup, "He must have gotten knocked into Repeat Mode!"

Buttercup trotted over to Buzz.

"Buttercup, you are the coolest unicorn in the universe," Buttercup said, grinning.

"Buttercup, you are the coolest unicorn in the universe," Buzz repeated.

The gang erupted in laughter.

"I'm not listening to this," Mr Potato Head said, yanking out his ears.

"What do we do?" Rex whined.

It was a good question. Jessie had asked the friends to take care of Buzz. Now he was worse off than when she left!

"We're gonna have to jiggle his wires," Hamm sighed."Before Bonnie gets home!" Trixie added.

"Before Jessie gets home," said Hamm.

Time was running out. The toys had to do something – and fast! "How do we 'jiggle' him?" Slinky asked.

Hamm thought a moment. "Bounce him on the bed, I guess."

The toys hauled Buzz onto the bed. "Jump!" Hamm said.

"A infinidad..." Buzz said as he bounced.

"Oh, boy," Hamm muttered. Then he told Rex to give his biggest jump. They needed to change something! Rex jumped. *Boing!* Buzz flew right off the bed!

Buzz landed facedown on the floor. The toys jumped down to help, but he didn't budge. They rolled him over, they tickled him, they yelled at him. Still, Buzz remained motionless.

Hamm glared at Rex. "Now what did you do?"

"I just did what you said!" Rex cried frantically.

The toys paused, horrified. Then they heard the car pull into the driveway.

"They're home!" yelled Mr Pricklepants. The Peas hopped into their pod and hid.

"Hurry – we've got to fix Buzz!" Hamm shouted.

Rex undid Buzz's back panel and stared at a mass of wires.

"Which one?" Rex asked. "The red or the blue?"

Hamm looked at the wires and guessed. "Uh, blue then red!"

"No! Red then *black*!" cried Mr Potato Head. "Hurry!"

There was a noise outside the door. The toys went limp just as Bonnie's mother walked in and put down Bonnie's backpack. The room was a mess!

"Bonnie!" Bonnie's mum started down the hall. "Please come clean up this room!"

"It *is* clean, Mum!" Bonnie called from the kitchen.

"Buzz, are you okay?" Jessie asked as she jumped out of Bonnie's backpack. Woody and Dolly were right behind her.

"Oh, uh, he's fine." Trixie propped Buzz into a sitting position. Buzz fell over with a *thunk*.

"It's not my fault!" Rex wailed. "There are too many wires!"

Jessie shook her head and laughed. Then she whacked Buzz on the back. Buzz blinked and looked at his friends.

"Do I have something on my face?" he asked.

The other toys sighed with relief. Buzz was back to normal!

"All right, all right, everyone!" Woody said. "Now let's fix this room before Bonnie comes back!" The toys went into action to tidy up.

Minutes later, Bonnie walked into her room. "Mum sure is picky," she said. Everything was perfectly tidy, just the way she had left it.

Then she picked up Buzz. "Thanks for looking after everyone, Buzz.

I knew this place would be okay with you in charge!"

SHOWTIME!

After Andy's toys had settled into their new home in Bonnie's room, Dolly announced that she had a plan to help everyone get to know one another better. "Let's have a talent show!" she said.

All the toys were excited. They couldn't wait
to share their talents.

As everyone else started practising songs, building sets and memorizing lines, Buzz Lightyear stood by himself, thinking. His friends all seemed to know exactly what to do, but he wasn't sure.

He knew he was talented. After all, he was Buzz
Lightyear, Space Ranger. He had plenty of skills! But which
ones should he show off? He wanted to perform something
truly spectacular, amazing and different – something that
would impress Jessie the cowgirl.

Suddenly, he noticed Hamm and Buttercup working on their comedy routine. Buzz knew that Jessie loved a good joke. If he was in their act, she would see how funny he was!

"I can do impressions," Buzz announced as he joined his friends. Grabbing Woody's hat, he shouted, "Howdy partners, I'm Sheriff Woody. Did you know there's a snake in my boot?"

"I don't know about sounding like Woody," said Hamm with a smirk, "but you definitely sound *wooden*."

Buzz wasn't paying attention, though. He'd just noticed that Mr Pricklepants and the Aliens were practising a play. "Jessie loves to watch plays!" Buzz thought to himself, hurrying over.

The Aliens were very excited about their show, which Mr Pricklepants was directing. The hedgehog even invited Buzz to join the cast. "There are plenty of parts," Mr Pricklepants said encouragingly. "We're doing a classic: *Romeo and Juliet*!"

"That sounds great!" replied Buzz. "But don't you think the play would be much better if we made a few changes? I know! Let's create a new version – *Romeo and Juliet... In Space!*"

For once, Mr Pricklepants didn't know what to say.

Just then, Buzz heard Jessie's voice. "Well, I think you're a fantastic space ranger!"

Buzz thought Jessie was talking to him – but when he turned to respond, she was already walking away. She had been complimenting Rex, who was reenacting scenes from his favourite Buzz Lightyear video game with Trixie.

Rex was frowning, though. "I just feel like something's missing," he told Trixie.

Buzz stepped forward. "Maybe that something is me!"

The dinosaurs were thrilled to have the real Buzz in their act. "Wait till Jessie sees me do this!" Buzz smiled to himself, imagining how Jessie would enjoy his space ranger moves. He demonstrated his karate chop, swept his laser around the room and leaped off the furniture, shouting, "To infinity, and beyond!"

Buzz finished his space ranger routine proudly.

But Rex and Trixie just stared. "That's not what happens in the game," Rex whispered to Trixie.

At that moment, Slinky Dog called out to the space ranger. "Hey, Buzz! Take a look at that fancy footwork!"

Buzz looked over and saw Woody and Bullseye practising their riding and roping routine. He had to agree. They were very good at rodeo tricks.

Then it struck him – what if he could do a cool trick of his own? Jessie would love that!

Seeing the Peas-in-a-Pod nearby, Buzz asked, "Anyone need a lift?"

The Peas bounced into his hands, and Buzz started juggling them. To make his act more exciting, Buzz added some other tricks, too!

"Hey, guys! Time to start the show!" shouted Dolly.

As the other toys rushed to their seats, Jessie called, "Come on, Buzz! Are you ready? I can't wait to see your act!"

Buzz's smile froze. "Oh, no!" he muttered anxiously. He still hadn't decided which act to do!

Up on the stage, Bullseye turned on the music.

A lively, upbeat tune filled the room... and suddenly, Buzz's whole body shook.

Then his foot began twitching. Then his arm. The Peas jumped out of the way as Buzz's body began to twist, too.

It was as if the music was taking over his body!

Unable to control himself, Buzz started dancing. He couldn't stop!

He danced all the way across the room, straight to Jessie. Then he grabbed her and dipped her almost to the ground.

"Uh, I-I don't know why I did that," Buzz apologized, blushing. "I couldn't help myself!"

But Jessie grinned. She knew exactly what had happened – the music had switched Buzz into his Spanish Mode!

"It's okay, Buzz," she whispered. "Just go with it!"

Buzz smiled shyly back at Jessie. "Um, well then," he said. "May I have this dance?"

When Jessie nodded, the two danced up and across the stage. They dipped and twirled. They swung and whirled. And they smiled at each other the whole time.

All their friends clapped and cheered.

When the music finally ended, Buzz and Jessie took a bow together.

Buzz was beaming. He'd finally impressed Jessie, discovered a talent he never knew he had and found the new and spectacular act he'd been looking for! What a great way to kick off the talent show!

Disney · PIXAR

TOY STORY 3

WILD WEST SHOWDOWN!

From atop a high cliff, Sheriff Woody watched a train rumble across the desert.

Suddenly – KA-BLAM! The roof of one of the train cars exploded. The outlaw One-Eyed Bart climbed out, carrying bags of stolen money.

Woody grabbed his lasso and leapt into action.

"You've got a date with justice, One-Eyed Bart!"
cried Sheriff Woody.

The surprised bandit stopped in his tracks and
dropped the bags of money at Woody's feet.

"Ai-ai-ai-ai-ai-yah!" came a cry from behind Woody. It was One-Eyed Betty – One-Eyed Bart's karate-chopping wife!

Betty charged, knocking Woody right off the train.

"Ahh!" cried Woody.

Suddenly, Jessie the cowgirl came speeding up on her trusty steed, Bullseye. They caught Woody just in time!

"Give it up, Bart!" Woody called. "You've reached the end of the line."

But One-Eyed Bart wouldn't be stopped that easily. He pulled out a detonator and pressed the button.

KA-BooM! A bridge across a giant canyon was blown to pieces.

Bart and Betty jumped into their getaway car.

"It's me or the kiddies!" yelled One-Eyed Bart. "Take your pick!"

As the outlaws sped away, Jessie looked up and saw that the train was filled with orphans – and it was heading right towards the blown-up bridge!

"Ride like the wind, Bullseye!" Woody shouted. He
had to save the orphans before going after One-Eyed Bart.
When the brave horse reached the front of the train,
Woody leapt onto the engine.

"Hurry!" yelled Jessie. The train was speeding towards the canyon!

Woody quickly found the brake and pulled on it as hard as he could.

The train came to a screeching halt – but not
soon enough. It plummeted into the canyon with
Woody and the orphans still on board.

"No!" Jessie cried.

Suddenly, Buzz Lightyear the space ranger appeared!
He flew beneath the train and lifted it out of the canyon.

"Glad you could catch the train, Buzz!" shouted Woody.

Jessie and Bullseye cheered with delight as Buzz carried
the train to safety.

"Now let's catch some criminals!" said Buzz.

Buzz swooped down and used his laser to slice
One-Eyed Bart's getaway car in two. Bart, Betty and
their Alien sidekicks tumbled out onto the ground.

Suddenly, a giant dog with a metal coil for a body surrounded the outlaws.

"You can't touch me, Sheriff!" shouted One-Eyed Bart. "I brought my attack dog with a built-in force field!"

"Well, I brought my dinosaur, who eats force-field dogs!" replied Woody.

"Yodel-lay-hee-hooooooo!" yodelled Jessie.

A gigantic dinosaur burst out of the ground with a ferocious ROAR!

But before the dinosaur could attack, a giant shadow appeared overhead. A pig-shaped spaceship beamed One-Eyed Bart, Betty and their sidekicks to safety.

"Evil Dr Porkchop!" cried Woody.

"That's Mister Evil Dr Porkchop to you!" yelled the villain from behind the control panel. With a wicked laugh, Dr Porkchop pressed a button and dropped an army of vicious monkeys onto Woody, Jessie and Buzz.

"Buzz!" shouted Woody above the screeching monkeys. "Shoot your laser at my badge!"

"Woody, no!" cried Buzz. "It will kill you!"

"Just do it!" yelled Woody.

Buzz aimed his laser beam at Woody's badge and fired. The beam bounced off the badge and hit Dr Porkchop's spaceship. BOOM!

Soon the villains were all tied up and ready to go to jail.
"Good job, deputies!" Woody shouted. The Sheriff and
his friends had saved the day again!

I finished
this book on

....

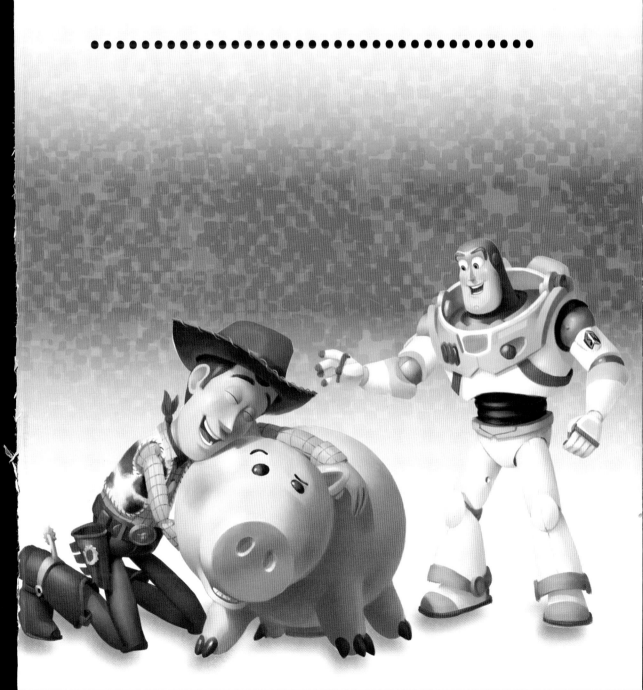

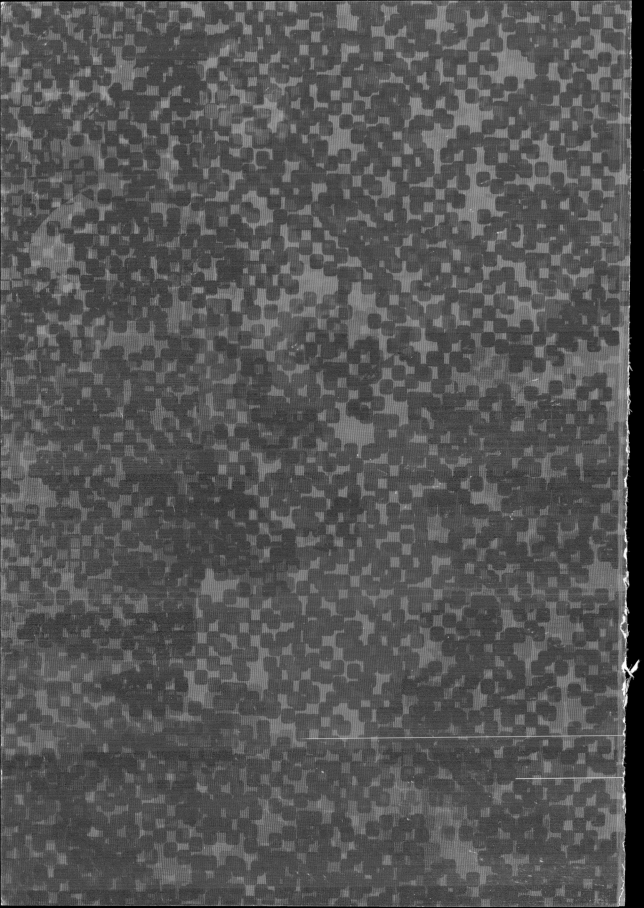